TEN POETS
Get to the Bottom of Some Grisly Crimes

G.B. Clarkson • Anne-Laure Coxam • Livia Franchini
Mathew Lyons • Helena Nelson • Luke Palmer
Ilse Pedler • Nathaniel Spain • Chloe Stopa-Hunt
Erica Wright

TEN POETS

POETS

Get to the Bottom of Some Grisly Crimes

selected and edited by
Jon Stone and Kirsten Irving

sidekickBOOKS

First published in 2024 by
SIDEKICK BOOKS
www.sidekickbooks.com

Printed by 4edge Limited

Typeset in Libre Baskerville and Manrope

Copyright of text and images remains with the authors.

Kirsten Irving and Jon Stone have asserted their right to be
identified as the editors of this work under Section 77 of the Copyright,
Designs and Patents Act 1988.

All rights reserved.

No part of this book may be reproduced, stored in a
retrieval system or transmitted in any form without
the written permission of Sidekick Books.

Cover design / typesetting by Jon Stone
ISBN: 978-1-909560-35-2

Cover: 'Last Respects to the Remains of Counts Egmont and Hoorn' by
Louis Gallait, 1859 / Source: Wikimedia Commons

Foreword

"But wait an instant!", as Sherlock Holmes exclaims in *The Hound of the Baskervilles*. Wondering further on what we have promised on the cover to this book, we find ourselves interrogating its very premise. Are a poet and a detective not totally unlike one another? Where the detective sets out to present a solution, to grapple with an open case until it is closed, the poet is of a mind to take what is closed and re-open it, to pursue the question over the answer. Also, as Holmes adds, moments after the aforequoted line, "It is the first quality of a criminal investigator that he should see through a disguise." But poets *love* disguises; they dote on what could be, what is merely suggested. They delight in the surface of things – especially the surface of language, which is their chief material, in the same way a pastry chef is concerned with casings, glazings and frostings. It is of some irritation to their critics that they are reluctant to put aside this fascination and use their facility with words to instead point the finger, firmly and justly. Where they might pull back the curtain, they instead ask you to touch its fabric, to feel its ripple.

But then again... then again, while fictional detectives nearly always crack the puzzle presented to them, the best of them remain troubled by the deeper mysteries surrounding it. Holmes again, at the close of *The Adventure of the Cardboard Box*:

> What object is served by this circle of misery and violence and fear? It must tend to some end, or else our universe is ruled by chance, which is unthinkable. But what end? "

Many a sleuth has followed in Holmes' stead, staring moodily out across moorlands, coastal cliffs, cityscapes or harbours, at times dwelling on the dark side of their professional success – how it's owed to the inability of intelligent men and women to correct the circumstances which give rise to murderous instincts. The detective story may, mechanically speaking, be an elaborate self-solving problem – a Rubik's cube that twists and turns until colours on all sides are aligned – but it has also proven to be a reliable vehicle for meditations on the misshapen human soul. The grim violations and macabre scenes that sit at the centre of their plots are provocations which are not entirely neutralised by the catching of the culprit, or the assurance that said culprit will go to meet their own bleak fate. This being the case, the poet's preoccupation with mask and window dressing, with the peripheral and the astray, has a part to play alongside the detective's more direct concern with 'the facts', and ought to be considered part of a much broader ongoing psychological investigation. Indeed, the poet would make a formidable sidekick to the dogged gumshoe in all of us – and it should come as no surprise that the editors of this press rather warm to that idea.

Isn't it also the case, come to think of it, that the foolishness of poets closely echoes the apparent eccentricity of the most famous fictional detectives, who often appear, in the eyes of baffled policemen and doctors, to waste time rummaging in odd corners, seaching through their own pockets, or asking banal questions of irreproachable witnesses? Ever since the creation of Edgar Allen Poe's C. Auguste Dupin, the secret weapon of this character archetype has been imaginative resourcefulness – being prepared to think, look and act in ways that others dismiss, and in doing so discover new passageways through the darkness. One real-life detective – Frances Glessner Lee, renowned citizen criminologist of 1950s Chicago – became a pioneer of modern forensic pathology when she began constructing elaborate replications of crime scenes in the style of doll houses. Of these 'nutshell studies' she said:

> Each model is a tableau depicting the scene at the most effective moment (...) The investigator may best examine them by imagining himself a trifle less than six inches tall. With that firmly in mind, a few moments of observation will then make him able to step into the scene and there find many tiny details that might otherwise escape notice. "

Now, Watson, tell me: what does this remind you of?

Contents

G.B. CLARKSON
Our Client Sat Up With Staring Eyes
— In which holy vows meet most unholy secrets...
p. 12

ANNE-LAURE COXAM
The Capricorn king and the Tobacco queen can't bear grisly crimes
— In which two displaced wanderers find the truth an elusive subject...
p. 20

LIVIA FRANCHINI
The Dragoon Affair
— In which Mary Shelley relates a most regrettable incident involving two poets and a policeman...
p. 26

MATHEW LYONS
The Girl with the Golden Thread
— In which delicate bones are found cradled in a crypt...
p. 34

HELENA NELSON
Who Killed Search Party?
— In which a promising sophomore sings a swan-song...
p. 38

LUKE PALMER
Lateral Foot Pain as Caged Psychopath
— In which a conversation between familiars starts to muzzle both parties...

p. 42

ILSE PEDLER
A Windermere Murder
— In which a local beauty is suffocated before millions of witnesses...

p. 46

NATHANIEL SPAIN
Woodwake
— In which a body is found in the forest, and payment is made...

p. 50

CHLOE STOPA-HUNT
Margosha
— In which parts must be gathered, healed and put back together...

p. 52

ERICA WRIGHT
Search & Rescue
— In which a volunteer examines a crime scene and finds part of herself there...

p. 60

Appendix:
Megadetective vs the Megamurderscene
p.62

About the Authors / P.I. Directory
p.65

G.B. Clarkson

Our Client Sat Up With Staring Eyes

ANTEROOM

A robin twitches sideways on a twig. *Let me spill liquid into (the bud of) your swollen ear*. His breast bleeds. Aunt X, related to Sister Z, reads with a lilting accent, interposing frequently – *oh listen to this!* Sauveur, savour, a long track leading back to the city; sparks coming off a smelting works nearby. Cherry blossom sprinkled all over the rail tracks; spring killed.

> *Beads on the trees*
> *by the lees of the Thames:*
> *rimy*

Inside the enclosure of the monastery – or moanery, as we call it – it's Tuesday morning and there's a demon giving a demonstration. *How to / How not to*. His bare back is hedged with coarse fur, tawny like autumn.

Only the Cellarer is exempt from attending the talk, browsing among her mallets, hammers and fiddlery; stocking up; stocking down (this last due to *laissez-faire* and weak elastic, but the porn cliché clings, like a novice to her censored mail).

She prepares for her weekly inspection, with the robin as batman.

IN THE FRONT PARLOUR

"My dear Watson, you know how bored I have been since we locked up Colonel Carruthers. My mind is like a racing engine, tearing itself to pieces because it is not connected up with the work for which it was built. Life is commonplace, the papers are sterile, audacity and romance seem to have passed for ever from the criminal world."

Watson, sipping from a cheap teacup, toys with a hoop-shaped biscuit and the notion of summoning the Portress for more; contemplates summer outside the window: the slow bikers and pocket-spirited amblers of Marylebone. "Things are in the saddle, Holmes," he quotes, stirring. A sugary half-hoop revolves and dissolves in a tannin vortex.

IN THE COMMUNITY ROOM

Ten Mothers in twelve circles discuss internal affairs. Their knotted twine of the macramé binds them together.

IN THE LAUNDRY

Over the course of a month, a member of the community has discovered, in the overflow sink, four unexpected members: a pair of forearms, praying; and two thighs, crossed. The Monastic Council was called in, and employed chisels and pliers to prise apart the praying, crossed limbs – which turned out not, in fact, to be pairs – mystical wedding bands on both ring fingers, and thighs disparately suede-fleshed and bony. "Get to the bottom of it," Mother Assistant says bluntly, abandoning the Laundry Mistress to an almighty jumble of unnamed knickers.

IN THE KITCHEN

Congealed eggs and carp's roe are inspected for traces of arsenic. Butternuns prepare croûtons, insouciant.

IN THE WORKROOM

Officers sift through old lace and torn scapulars.

ON THE LANDING

Novices – unable to chatter – tumble to chapel, yanking white cowls, which they kiss, from hooks *en route*, attending to candlesticks as they pass.

IN THE CLOISTER

Some sisters wait (some wait years) for the bell to sound for chapel.

IN THE CHAPEL

The best chantresses sing shorter and shorter. Rubberneckers peer through the laity grille. There's a knife in the descant.

IN THE GALLERY

A Sister intones alone in a foreign language, interspersed with heart-cries and *"Écoutez! Écoutons!"*

IN THE GARDEN

Leaden skies. Sisters hitch up habits and weed. They converse in a non-particular way. No mention of murder aloud.

IN THE GARTH

The lime-fronded tomb of the Foundress awaits exhumation – part of the beatification process.

IN THE REFECTORY

French bowls are lifted to decorous, desiccated lips. St Benedict used to bless himself to avoid being poisoned. A delicious soupçon of sherry on a feast day loosens tongues to tell of midnight pausings in the corridors. An intruder leapt upon in the lobby, crying for mercy. A convent where all the Sisters were possessed. Sharp little serpent heads lifting in the breast. And this latest: dismemberment, onsite.

IN THE CELLS

Attending officers are wrongfooted by each Sister calling her cell 'our cell', in the spirit of poverty and the common life, and to avoid implication of ownership: "I was in our cell all evening, Officer." "I was reading the Divine Office, Officer."

IN THE INFIRMARY

Infirmarians administer small doses of morphine to the more irascible elderly nuns, who go off with a whimper. Numbers dwindle but no one minds. New flocks of postulants arrive each week, drawn by features in the Sunday papers, to replace those who have departed.

IN THE LIBRARY

Despite instructions from superiors to regard the police officers' questions like those of the priest in Confession, and not to throw shade on the Community, Sister Rubecula sings like a canary. She tells detectives that seven middle-aged, seasoned sisters had an experience years ago in the old Library (no longer used). They'd stumbled across a glowing, cocoon-shaped object – some sort of mummy – in a clearing by *Desert Fathers*. Seemingly without substance, its glow had mesmerised them, and for this they had neglected refectory and office bells, immured themselves, turned thin and abstracted, unable to wrench themselves away. After unsuccessful remonstrations, the monastery's hierarchy had given up both on them and on book-learning, and had had the old Library bricked up from the outside.

IN THE CRYPT

Investigating officers find torn-off fingers, fungus, dried eyes, obscurely-stained rags, viscera etcetera – each labelled with a name from the local martyrology.

EXIT

Police authorities arranged for the wall to be dismantled, the bricks dislodged like sulky teeth from gaping gums. Inside, they found eight female skeletons, arrested in bolt-upright sitting positions, four-by-four, skull-to-skull, against ramshackle shelves, amidst scattered serge cloths, bird beaks and small mammal bones. The room swam with ashy dust drifting and tunnelling in darling shafts of pale daylight, and one policeman said he'd found God.

(The title and 'My dear Watson' speech are quoted from 'The Adventure of Wisteria Lodge' and 'The Case of Colonel Carruthers' by Sir Arthur Conan Doyle.)

Anne-Laure Coxam

*The Capricorn king and the Tobacco queen
can't bear grisly crimes*

so they sip
some herby
aqua vitae

she caresses his ankles
he caresses her ears

they glide over the abyss
slip into margins
vanish into cracks

reappear dressed-up
with poems in their pockets

*

one of those nights
the Tobacco queen asked

    why not forget the investigation once and for all?

> well, because we don't know how to
> and what would we do anyway?

joy!
she exclaimed

> I don't do joy
> he replied

no, me neither
she admitted

*

How do they investigate crimes so terrifying? So terrifying they are dreading solving them? It is tedious. The investigation is oblique. They keep good relationships with witnesses but never question them unless they are dead

drunk

that night

they buried evidence under the roses. They shredded clues into confetti. They drank and made their love to forget *and* to remember.

In the morning the Capricorn king cooked hard-boiled eggs with asparagus.

*

yet the Tobacco queen dives into the lake
at the bottom of the abyss

> when she swims back to the surface
> she spits out bones onto the grass

the Capricorn king picks up
the bones from the grass

the Capricorn king sends the bones
to the Sphinx Forensic Laboratory

the Lab opens at odd hours
leaves no paper trail
only speaks on the phone
the Lab too is oblique
the Lab likes poetry

> which is not surprising
> from an institution
> that makes sense
> of bodies in various states
> of decomposition

*

In his past, the Capricorn king travelled. One day, he was asked to dig out a line of dusty rhododendrons along a driveway. Dry wind and dust. Dusty king with a pickaxe. Pickaxe on dusty ground and taproots running deep. Deep. To the centre of the earth.

The king cried over his pickaxe, his pickaxe digging out the endless taproots, the crime pickaxing at his mind (it was a clue, of course).

In her past, the Tobacco queen followed many leads haphazardly before moving to Scotland. In Scotland, she rested on the damp grass under a clotheshorse before moving in a tenement. In this flat, she lost a lot of blood, a lot of blood dripped on the wooden floors. The blood was a resurgence of the crime (obviously).

*

       were you dreaming?

asked the Forensic Lab
when the Tobacco queen
picked up the phone at 3am
she said she wasn't

the Lab said

       never mind

       check your emails
       I sent you something

they hung up
an email
it was unusual

*

the Capricorn king and the Tobacco queen's encounter
was an explosion
a breakthrough
in the investigation

they ventured down the abyss and found the lake
at the bottom of the abyss

they found shelter in each other's body
they felt the danger of this venture

they knew the bodies
hidden at the bottom of the lake
they knew monsters guarded them

it made them pause

compelling evidence
was hidden in the lake

getting closer to the crime
made them want to escape
made them want to dive deeper

*

She checked her emails. The Lab had sent a picture of the French writer Georges Perec, along with pictures of the bones they had found in the lake.

She said to the Capricorn king

> you know, I read somewhere
> ChatGPT can't write a sentence
> without any 'e' as Georges Perec did
>
> > is it true?
>
> I don't know
>
> > it can't be Georges Perec in the lake
> > can it?
>
> no it can't be
>
> > it might be a mistake

It was no mistake (the Lab doesn't make mistakes) but they looked at each other and silently agreed to delete the email.

they felt
relieved
they had reached
another dead end

and

she caressed his ankles
he caressed her ears

Livia Franchini

The Dragoon Affair

[ALIBI]

Illustrious –
 we ignore how or wherefrom these events came to pass between us and Sargent Masi, and we deeply regret them.

For we did not happen to be on the city road, returning from our friend's shooting range, where he – respected aristocrat from Britain and world-renowned poet – enjoys passing his afternoons shooting at silver guineas lodged in bamboo canes, encouraging his slim, intellectual friends to join him in a game in which he always wins.

We empathise with poor Masi's sorrowful state and wish him soon restored to full health.

We were all at home or far behind when it happened.

[UNBEARABLE]

I left our darkened flat at dawn to get apples.

We have agreed the safest thing is to stay in during the day until our names are cleared.

The grocer said the man was pierced side-to-side by the three spears, and it's a miracle he's still alive.

In town they say they saw a man throw the rake from Byron's doorstep.

I haven't told the boys, to avoid further hysterics.

Percy forgets to eat.

[INVISIBLE CITIZENS]

This Italian city we've perched ourselves in puzzles us, though we persist.

Flat and full of damp, except on mornings when the sun rises up fast, and it is easy to picture our group of flats along the river ascending, like futuristic treehouses, connected by the fairylight filaments of our thoughts. We are convinced we are birds. These mornings make the rest of our days make sense.

Percy and I are most content to exist in our nest.

(The townspeople here know nothing of our brilliant minds and notice us only for our difference. The women wear skirts so long they trail behind them in the rain. I do not mean to be unkind. To put it simply, we do not speak the same language.)

[APPLES]

They're all that Percy'll have, and only if the woman slices them thinly and soaks the slices briefly in milk.

I fear he's going mad with guilt.

At least, the grocer says, the man still lives.

[DAY OUT]

We ride back in the evening between five and six.

Five English poets on five Italian rental horses.

Six, if you count the one attached to the carriage transporting us literary ladies, our men's heroic exploits imprinted upon our retinae.

Our men are famously mild-mannered.

They only ever handle guns at shooting ranges.

We are otherwise a peaceable community of lettereds.

[UNDER ATTACK]

The grocer says that within a quarter of a mile of Porta le Piaggie, they were overtaken by a man on horseback.

The dragoon was riding at full gallop, red and black like a fury, swollen with wine and laughter, with darkened teeth in a face flushed bright, on a white stallion, in a cloud of dry dust, spooking poor John Taaffe's horse.

He looked a mad Hussar from his jacket, and above all, he looked just like a devil!

(Now they claim Mr Masi was merely in a rush to get back to work after his lunch break.)

[POOR JOHN TAAFFE]

And Taaffe, whom the Baron was always mocking for being a bad shooter, always accusing of riding in the silly manner of the Spanish –

Taaffe, among us the most talentless student, slaving away on his Dante –

Taaffe was knocked off his horse.

I, Mary Shelley, laughed, looking up from the porthole of our carriage.

He lost his head and went after the devil.

[IMPOSSIBLE]

For I cannot imagine the men who were with him – whoever was with Taaffe when he was attacked – would have reacted in any way other than level-headed, had they been Englishmen.

Given I can't imagine my husband would set on a wild chase after a man dressed in red, no matter how fearful he might have appeared in the first instance.

Granted that gentlemen from respectable backgrounds will always check whether a man in a uniform is a representative of a local branch of law enforcement and there's no chance they would mistake him for a bandit.

And since I couldn't see well from my position in the carriage...

It's impossible that one of our own could have mortally wounded a policeman for right of way on a public thoroughfare.

We very much enjoy living here in your city.

We call it our nest of singing birds.

Mathew Lyons

The Girl with the Golden Thread

Poor broken church. Norman tower. Gilbert Scott reredos and choir. *I can't believe you and I are so near.* White lime defacing the saints; the traces of a Doom above the chancel. *Old habits. I dipped my fingers in the font.* Angels roosting in the beams. Bats too: dark fruit in the dark ribs of an upturned hull. In the evening I felt them: a chill, wild movement shifting the air.

Was it once St Æthelwynn's? Allowing that she lived at all. Mercia's own, scraped from the skin of the chronicles. Now the developers are in: apartments and a penthouse for the east window; rose of the world. God's homeless again, sleeping in the trees for shelter.

Here, under the Saxon crypt, under the broken ochre of burnt Roman bricks, unknitted from their courses under trowelfuls of mud and time, I found you, *daughter*. Four thousand years on a raft of stone and clay, huddled bones beside the eternal gossip of a spring. *Find a church alone and far from its people; it'll have its feet in pagan water.* Oh, the reports I must complete because of you: red tape around the find scene – a bureaucracy of wonder. *This is process, though, and not a rite.*

A thought in my mind: a mouse, a stylus, scratching at something indistinct. *I can reach through the skin of the world to your bones, steep my hands in your death.* Vertebrae shattered at the neck – here between C1 and C2, atlas and axis, far apart. A death so naked it needs no reading at all. Water drips. Your remains cluster like clay markings. *One man's rite is murder, but a society's is sacrifice.*

The bones of your feet – cuneiform, metatarsal – splay like petals in the dirt. What was written in your death – a supplication, a summoning? Were you the gift? Was death the gift to you? *Which way does the power flow?* Were you a promise to the world that runs in the veins of the weather? Even now, are you in the blood of the moon and bough? Why else did they lie you – another Verbaek, on a bed of goose's wing – if not for migration. This world, that – something arrived, something departed. A rite and not a process. Why else the golden threads running through the lyre of your hand. What gorgeous cloth of knowing did you hold? Later, I'll scour the literature for analogues, precedents. There's nothing new, not even death.

A thought, a spider in my hair: how do you judge me, my child of raw dawns and naked darkness?

In the arc lights, late at night beside you, blinking in time's long unbearable gaze. Water drips. Whose ghosts are shuffling above me, penitents sailing into grace on the bow of the nave, shipping light at sunrise, listing into evening prayer? Thinking of Æthelwynn, wrecked on shoals of indifference. I still need to label your bones, catalogue you. A process, not a rite. How wrong is it – in the name of the god of information – to pull the dead from their beds like late sleepers and pack them for the laboratory, the radiography suite? *Let me hold the world of your skull, wild with knowledge: the ways of the living, the ways of the dead, hunger and starlight, grace and blood.*

I take the threads and hold them, radial lines on the tablet of my hand. Water drips. The lights are flickering. Every kind of wrong. *Something cold moving through the vault.* Something arrived. Something departed. *Which way does the power run?* Is every child a sacrifice on the altar of the world?

Helena Nelson

Who Killed Search Party?

What happened to *Search Party*, Richard Meier's second collection? The whereabouts of the body must be the first issue. Have you seen this book in a shop? Is the author's name familiar? Or the title? If the answer to these questions is 'no', premature death may be hypothesised. But why and how? Weapon, motive, opportunity – all are necessary.

One possible murder weapon was a notice in *Stride* in 2019, posted online just before the Covid pandemic descended. Few adults read books of poetry; fewer still seek out reviews. Unless, that is, the writer trashes his subject, as in this case. Thus: both opportunity and motive. The reviewer, a neglected poet, craves attention. Infuriated by the latest over-lauded invader, he seizes the chance to despatch him. What need for mercy? Perhaps the esteemed publisher (Picador) has rejected his own work in the past. Too lazy to invest much time, he poisons his headline with sarcasm ("Mind-blowing") and as he sums up, his cut is vicious: "I didn't bother to read any more of this," he tells us. "I have better things to do [...] The cricket's on television."

Was death instant? Probably not. It was a painful expiration, during which time the victim looked for help that did not come.

A second murder suspect, however, must be the publisher, who could have saved a life, and did not. Was not this an author who had previously – to considerable acclaim – taken the publisher's own debut prize? When the work of a celebrated author founders, editorial reputations suffer. A marketing team has invested in typesetting, jacket design, blurb-writers. Astonished by a brutal attack on their product, they must rally their troops. The series editor (a leading poet) is bound to summon emergency first-aid: new reviews that do not confuse opinion with fact. This did not happen. How very suspicious!

Nevertheless, the true murderer is rarely the first suspect, or even the second. Another option merits consideration. Did the author stifle his own book? Could it have been suicide? In its early pages (dismissed by the rogue reviewer as "quietly innocuous"), some indications support this theory. In 'Last Chance', for example, there are moving hints of panic and desperation. In 'Hell', the poet consults a dictionary of phobias, only to find that his "fear of things / is not a thing". Throughout the section titled 'Findings', a detached, clinical tone masks terrifying observations. The penultimate poem, 'On your cruelty', describes fatal damage to snow-covered trees and concludes: "In nature it occurs by accident" – a swift, iambic blow to the jugular. Could it be that Meier himself feared poems that spoke plainly of existential terror? Instead of leaving them to their dying throes, he could have defended them. He did not.

The penultimate poem, 'On your cruelty', describes fatal damage to snow-covered trees and concludes: "In nature it occurs by accident" – a swift, iambic blow to the jugular. Could it be that Meier himself feared poems that spoke plainly of existential terror? Intead of leaving them to their dying throes, he could have defended them. He did not. Perhaps he thought it was pointless. Perhaps some impulse in him had always courted failure as an art form. In 'The art of the through ball', he introduces a cricketer whose team-mates encourage safe batting. But the player's temptation is towards the unsafe, on grounds that it "might, if read, be beautiful". It might "open a defence, / that's slid to no one, into emptiness". With such play a cricketer might indeed score. But the phrase "if read" provides the necessary clue. A book that soars out of sight won't be read at all.

Nevertheless, such a "desolate pass" is hard to achieve in real life. In 1863, Emily Dickinson wrote to Thomas Wentworth Higginson: "Are you too deeply occupied to say if my verse is alive?" She enclosed four poems. If poems are alive to start with, they are hard to kill. A murderer may assault them. A publisher may assist. The author may bat them into emptiness. But send out your search party. *Search Party* lives.

Luke Palmer

Lateral Foot Pain as Caged Psychopath

A 4am hospital. Limp corridors. Doors that drip on
their hinges.
Mise en scene *inc. costume all once-white, now grey static.*
Behind a steel door: a cell. A chair faces it.
Sit down. A moment of silence.
Then...

Do you know who I am?

> I am the blue mountain.
> I am the coiled snake.
> I am glad you are here.

Do you know why I came?

I've seen both films. The second one got the eyes right
but the first had a more accurate mouth.

Turning on its bunk, it is all mouths, all red
and toothed, and all speaking at once.
What you'd thought was its back

is another mouth, closed.
Resist the urge to recoil.
More silence.
Then...

Can you help me?

>   Depends what you mean by *help*.
>   Depends what you mean by *me*.

Are you going to obstruct the investigation?

>   A man who cannot talk should ask better questions.

You remove the gag. A breath.
Remember to breathe.
It licks its lips.
Then...

Do you know what I will find if I keep looking?

>   A thousand needle points. A hammer. Wires.

Tell me about the wires.

Shifts on the mattress, voice tightening.

> Under the skin. But barely. Like veins running with copper or rust or sometimes choked with too much blood. But hurry. There is much to see and do. Listen to the rain at the window. Like a stoic. Like a lollard. I know you understand this.

You can tell what I am thinking?

> You are thinking there's some out-of-date co-codamol in the drawer of the bureau but you've got the school run in an hour. You are thinking that after her road-traffic accident, Frida Kahlo made three thousand drawings of her foot but maybe I can help you.

Lights glitch and depart. Upon their return, notice the chair has become a bed, the bed a chair. The bars are inside out.

What are you offering me?

    Stillness. A full-bodied experience. The chance
                                                for some
    alone-time. An interruption of the
                                        usual programming.

What if I don't want that?

    There's always a compromise.

Is there anything I can do to stop this?

    You know where the door is. And the window.
    And the disused elevator shaft.

Struggle against your bonds.
Then...

Will you ever let me go?

    I am not the one holding on.

Footsteps along the corridor. A face at the viewing hole.
The lights turn off, then on, then off again.

Ilse Pedler

A Windermere Murder

Warning: Contains upsetting scenes, strong language and broken promises.
Identities may have been changed in the writing of this poem.

Her body, a putrefying bluey-green in summer air,
black flies busying themselves in its skin of slime,
choking the throat with stagnant stench,
and in her mouth a crumpled note:

> *I have a bed but do not sleep*
> *I rise without being woken*
> *My face is wet, I do not weep*
> *I bend but am never broken*

Who is she who was once beautiful, who lies before
    us broken?

In Bowness, tourists queue for chips outside
    Vinegar Jones.
There are 36 flavours of ice-cream in the shop on the prom
and no one seems concerned about the loss.

What motive could there be for such a murder?

Ask the boats: first *Mary-Anne*, whose broad
    sweeps once cleaved
the surface, and who knew the victim in her youth; did
    she dance
with her once too often before she too became victim?

Or *Jane*, showing off her red stripes and new engine.
She and her friends stirred up dirt wherever they went,
got their motors trimmed for their trouble.
Revenge was mentioned at the time.

And those underworld figures who spend their days
in the gloom of half-lit alleyways
of weeds and sunken things, keels broken on rocks,
shattered ribs reaching to the green light above.

In sibilant whispers they chant:

> *we sisters of the secret depths*
> *bear witness to her final breaths*
> *to find the killer first reflect*
> *on who grows rich on beauty's death*

We turn to science for answers:

Water molecules are composed of two
hydrogen atoms and one oxygen –
oxygen is the difference between life and death.

We take samples, find that phosphorus and nitrogen have shouldered their way between, running off fields, dipping their toes before sliding in

and filthy mouths spew filthy waste through grilles
    of teeth,
belch denials to keep the greedy fed
– who stops the source?

She must have felt her breath tighten over time.

She who was birthed of two glaciers to the sound
    of winds
hurling their howls at an unpolished sky,
her beauty so clear it was transparent.

for thousands of years the space to breathe
the space to breathe for thousands of years

Nathaniel Spain

Woodwake

The boy was found in the woods.

No one asked, but I went. To the coppiced holt beyond the manor. To the green-shadowed dell where his body had lain. The susurrus of leaves and the croaking of toads: *requiem, requiem, requiem*.

When I returned, I said it was the work of a gentleman. A guest of our landlord, stalking the woods out of season. Perhaps he had mistaken the boy for a deer.

> I could have said that I sat with my hands in the loam. That a conker cracked open, leaking the timbre of trees. The mist-riddled sky inverted, converted, relating the act between branch and root. The gunshot; an upthrust of mouldering leaves. A bough falling heavy. A burst of red berries.
>
>> Two days the boy lay, beech and oak standing sentinel. Centipede and nematode in work of unmaking. A most holy communion: earth to earth, blood to blood.

Your kin should have left him, said the woods, branches scraping. *From this, you gain nothing. Our roots are starving. The beasts of the mulch writhe in their famine. There could yet have been life. From this, a resurrection.*

Instead I said I had deduced how it happened. The residue of gunpowder. The fine print of a boot.

The crowd went to the manor. Gravel path, marble statues. In a mahogany closet, dry blood hung on a jacket. A gentleman from London was up for the week. It was an accident, he said, and he was terribly sorry. The family gained twenty pounds, and a year's reprieve on rent.

Chloe Stopa-Hunt

Margosha

in which the poet finds something that was lost

> "You must call in a way that your spirit will want to return."
> – Joy Harjo

What sort of bed do you go to
tonight when thick dews first lick
and loosen earth into its wet-woe dark?

a sweet one –   honest paeony
carnation pulling up her petticoat and
ginger spinning sorry tales of love

    The street rocks in its moorings

I am the act of ashes
scent of mud sent to me scent of the lost

You! who come winged out of the dolorous mist!
    Contest in song all
virtue charity and grief

I am the heart in green leaves
hewed helpless before you
heedless at even your memory

    The circling dance comes slower than it should
Perhaps somebody knows what happened
clack of shoes in a pattern, in a pattern –

    what you leave behind
becomes a thing to weave into a web of gold
bafflement   drawings

    the empty bottles   and   the pink-stained bath
praise her for her ways
what else   princess

You are a guest
who asked for nothing
like this leaving

Nail down my door
death comes by the waft
long-looked-for breeze

desired and not deserved
how could I be so careless
all that's left's laments

and then no voice at all
for my loose pearl
dews are not fine enough

days are never fresh
where is the slaughter?
I will go there

in which the poet recognises her after a while

> "Pass me by! Oh pass me by!"
> – from *Death and the Maiden*

I do not recognise her. You who come winged
out of the morning mist
I heard your story first

my eyes closed at the dazzling sight
I knew a girl of flesh
the sad and sorry red of blood on sheets

mouth, tendon, everything
and I'd like that
like none of this – a shade of you, the least

fine flower failing me
who lingers like a lover
I am bewildered by you over and over again

Are you my pearl that I have mourned
spice in the wind
says yes

look at me lightly
remember when you were a girl with a girl's flesh
and not this petalled white that is soft and

hard at once, like milk held up
between the hands
of a great priest

Oh I have seen your gaze before
and I recognise it now
my noise of grief is gone

Dear fortune who has laid me on my back before you
and cut me open with
her meagre knife –   fall to

*in which the poet begins to understand the magnitude of
    the venture*

> *"[Pearl] has the feel of the real, as if genuine grief provided
> the impetus for such a poetic undertaking."*
> – Simon Armitage

I should care for your rank
but all I want's to reach you
dazed and dimmed heart

defies all else –
I will dash the rivers and the rocks
alone as I have no need of myself I would gladly be rid
    of it

it does me no service it gives me no help
I was the saddest jeweller in the world
when the lights went out

but you say

I cannot come   you say

you're not   the only one

is it spring is it midnight
there are no photographs
there is no moon

no desert here nor night
especial grace   enough
innocence   Death

is by nature a great loneliness
but here the flocks
of girls pretend

to circle up like migratory birds –
or I have yoked them with
a desperate love as if at last

I have the chance to bless
I promise these are soft wild words
like the incense in the wind

the glassy river never darkens
the girls in pearls
who did no wrong

smile on and on, I think
but it's hard to see their faces
all the sound is song

I want to drown at once and be
made still
to watch to hear is madness

inside me all strings yearn
to rove and rest
returning with whispers

perhaps not this world
the river brighter than sunlight
is not unkind to me

in which the poet understands, and wishes to mete out justice

> *"One imagines that her art is her shadow, as though, like Peter Pan's, it is sewn permanently to her feet."*
> – from *Where is Ana Mendieta?*

the answer comes when I take off my old skin and put it
    out with the garbage
hush
my hand itself

has told a few lies
yet I have decided
no vision is enough

gild each night as much as you need to
nothing to defy
empty music, empty wine, empty fires

she will suffer again her body split. Better grieve it. Not
    that. Elements unmade
a matter of routine, without marking. Only the mild
    love of the scalpel. I will
make some notes. Every name and particular feature,
    let's have it set down

give us back to the lark –
I want hope
who has that?

make a pact
where the broom blows
there is no help

I give you back to the larks
and the gulls
the answer is the gift

the answer is they hurt us
the answer is unstitched
the answer tall grass, black woods and the rivers where
   no one

looks, clay softer than a girl's palm
a cast-off gown
he did it and he's going down

But I want to know, how can I shed his blood?
   and you can only give her

               back to the lark

Erica Wright

Search & Rescue

Every flash of red against the green pines leaves you breathless, ready for a bloodstain or at least a sliver of nylon, something fluttering on a branch, a flag saying, *you're close, you're close*. But then there's the lone ear, and you hesitate. You check your bootlaces, admire a hawk. You find yourself shooing the others ahead with your new favourite phrase, *I'll catch up*.

You carry a knife, too. Sometimes if you press the blade into your palm, you stop thinking about the campfire strewn with metacarpals. Before becoming a searcher, you associated tendons with arthritis, the way it flares when the frost rolls in. Once, you thought frost was pretty. You thought the whole forest was pretty: all those elms in winter like cathedral spires reaching toward heaven.

You strain to recall why you volunteered in the first place. Was it the lure of believing in something? The thing is, if you find the body first, it's your responsibility. Not legally. The police will thank you for your service and send you on your way. But you wake some nights in the middle of a clearing, unsure how you got there, your own hand wrapped around somebody else's lifeless hand.

If you don't think that matters, hold fast to the last thing you remember in the woods: cleaning the dog's muzzle where she nosed her owner's head. Gentle as a mama licking her pup, you set her free. You watch her brown fur until it disappears into the distance, the vision so clear you cry out. Could something so devoted kill? Could somebody like you? You startle at your own possibility.

Appendix:
Megadetective vs the Megamurderscene

In pursuit of the ultimate match-up between man/woman and mystery, we have combined descriptive passages from a number of well-regarded detective stories. The results are in, and we present to you, in one corner, the *Megadetective*:

> An extraordinary looking short little girl of eighteen, olive-skinned like a Syrian, chewing on the remnants of a cigar, more like a boy than a girl. Hardly more than five feet, six foot, two-four inches, very tall and lean, he carried himself with great dignity and an air of casual untidiness. His head was exactly the shape of an egg, round as a bullet from a box of marbles, capped closely with a mass of white sparrow's nest hair coiling crisply at the temples and clasping the cheeks like folded wings. He had a long face, a long, spare, wide-browed face, not unlike a horse, a face as round and dull as a Norfolk dumpling, red as a tomato, with a fine scimitar of a nose and a slightly receding chin; he had eyes as empty as the North Sea, with corners that turned down. His moustache was very stiff and military. The neatness of his attire was almost incredible; he was dressed in a shabby old kimono, a rumpled raincoat, and a black brocade dress, very much pinched in round the waist. Iron muscles shaped his jacket sleeves. Behind tortoiseshell-rimmed spectacles, the fierce, fearless, foolish, golden, faded blue grey eyes of a hawk sparkled with anticipation, lit with a spark of determination.

His hands and voice and phantom arm were grand. He wore something more than self-confidence but less than pride, a good deal blunted by rough contact with the world.

Confronting the detective, the *Megamurderscene*:

> The apartment was in the wildest disorder – the furniture broken and thrown about in all directions. It was vast, old-fashioned, high-ceilinged and not too well lit. A heavy smell of gunpowder and tobacco hung in the hallway. Upon the floor were found floor cushions, an ear-ring of topaz, a sharp shaft of moonlight, a white powdery substance, the cocktail tray, and two bags, containing nearly four thousand francs in gold, upon a thick pinkish Chinese rug. On a small table near the fireplace were pen and ink and a cremation certificate form. The bathroom was in no way remarkable. On a sort of low dais, the body of an old man lay like a grotesque full-sized puppet, at right angles to the gong, one beautiful hand shining like ivory, in a yellow dressing-gown with a very vivid scarlet lining, the feet splayed outwards, a hole in his scalp – nearly impossible to find even if you knew what you were looking for. There was a smear or so of blood, though very little. The man had, for a moment, placed his red hand on the wall. The hilt of a dagger stood up, black and shining, like a little horn, or a grave marker. The photographers clustered around the body, and the flashes grew more frequent. Someone was signalling from the tower;

a light there flashed every now and again. The panes were of frosted glass; the frame wide enough to admit a man's body. Beyond there was no other sound, no cars, no siren – just the rain beating.

What will our detective do next? Which methods will he use? Which clue is of most importance? Is anyone in the immediate vicinity a suspect? Will one of this book's poet-detectives (see opposite page onward) roll up to play the part of rival, associate or love interest?

SOURCES: *The Black Dudley Murder* by Margery Allingham; *Gin and Daggers: A Murder, She Wrote Mystery* by Donald Bain; *Five Go To Smuggler's Top* by Enid Blyton; *The Cloven Foot* by M.E. Braddon; *The Big Sleep* by Raymond Chandler. *The Innocence of Father Brown* by G.K. Chesterton; 'The Tuesday Night Club' by Agatha Christie; *The Mysterious Affair at Styles* by Agatha Christie; *Murder on the Links* by Agatha Christie; *Cover Her Face* by P.D. James; *The Secret of the Old Clock* by Carolyn Keene; *The Dean's Death* by Alfred Lawrence; *The Yellow Room* by Gaston Leroux; *A Man Lay Dead* by Ngaio Marsh; *The Long Arm of Gil Hamilton* by Larry Niven; *The Pilgrim of Hate* by Ellis Peters; 'The Murders in the Rue Morgue' by Edgar Allen Poe; *Whose Body?* by Dorothy L. Sayers; *Pietr the Latvian* by Georges Simenon; *The Yellow Dog* by Georges Simenon; *The Devil's Flute Murders* by Seishi Yokomizo.

About the Authors / P.I. Directory

G.B. CLARKSON (working name Candida Gumshoe Swirls) is a sticky-handed, *very* private detective with a knack for hacking doorbell cameras in the vicinity of crime scenes and clocking items carelessly dropped in nearby parks and gardens. She keeps trophies from previous cases wrapped in layers of cellophane inside a Galway shawl in her midtown offices, and is obsessive about her late father's collection of forensic specimens, including, it is said, odd eyeballs stilled in shocked final glances, bobbing in ethanol. Her unofficial assistant, Butterfingers, has sole access to her refrigerated outhouses and arranges all local and foreign travel. No animals are allowed on the premises and the detective has a gift for disarming potential suspects' defences by polka-dancing in a soft white fur bolero while singing in Gaelic.
@gbclarkson

ANNE-LAURE COXAM was brought up by repentant criminal Brandon the Badger, who had left his troubled past and terrible misdeeds behind. In redemption for his crimes, he turned Anne-Laure Coxam into a tireless crime fighter, teaching her to track down poems in the undergrowth and solve bloody cases by reading the signs in the mud. Nowadays, because of her ability to make herself invisible when shadowing, and her cat-like aura, it's not unusual for strangers in shady pubs, night buses,

dark streets and commuter trains to spontaneously stroke her hair.
IG: *@annelaurecoxam*

Hailing from Tuscany, her roots intertwined with ancient Etruscan soil, Detective LIVIA FRANCHINI emerges as a spectral figure in the city's heart—part investigator, part weaver of tales—haunting the shadows in relentless pursuit of truth. With a mastery of linguistic puzzles, she excels at unlocking the cryptic messages hidden within the urban sprawl, revealing the clandestine machinations lurking beneath the surface.
IG: *@livfranchini*

MATHEW LYONS thought he had quit the shamus game, but then a dame showed up on his doorstep with a dead body and a trowel.

"They say dead men tell no tales," he said.

"Not the ones I know," she said. "They never stop talking."
www.mathewlyons.co.uk

HELENA MARPLE NELSON resides in Fife. She has studied poetry, largely unobserved, for seven decades. Through the imprint HappenStance Press, she cultivates poets both alive and dead, thus enriching a number of poetic reputations. She is sometimes glimpsed at public events wearing a furry hat and gloves, and carrying a handbag, or small, mauve backpack, in which she keeps her notes.
www.happenstancepress.com / Twitter: *@nell_nelson*

LUKE PALMER is resigned to the fact this job will destroy him one day. He trains rookies by dint of poor example and has lost several on their first week in the job. His office has three layers of Venetian blinds and his desk drawers clink. He has a filing cabinet full of anglepoise lamps, all stamped CASE CLOSED in chocolate sauce, which, on grainy black-and-white film stock, has the look and texture of blood.
Twitter: *@lcpalmerpoet* / *lukepalmerwriting.com*

ILSE PEDLER is an eco-sleuth who may be spotted in waterproofs and well-worn walking boots tramping about the Lake District looking for evidence of ecological misdemeanour. Her assistant Gwen the Jack Russell, often seems more interested in posing on rocks for her many admirers and has to be occasionally reminded to focus on the job of hunting for clues. Gwen can be contacted via Instagram (*@IlsePedler*) or *ilsepedler.com/about/*
Also recommended: *www.savewindermere.com/*

NATHANIEL SPAIN's methods may be unconventional, but he gets the job done. When he's not at his desk, you can find him scouring the muddy banks of the Tyne for clues. Unearth his previous exploits in *Unfurl* (The Braag, 2023), *Carmina* Magazine, *Gastropoda*, *Carmen et Error* and *Provenance Journal*. His case files are archived at *www.nathanielspain.co.uk*.

CHLOE STOPA-HUNT solves best by moonlight. Controversial for her willingness to consult with psychics, she specialises in cases of sedition, bigamy

and blackmail – murder, she has been known to say, palls after your fifth. In another century, she'd have been put to the flames; happily, in this one, she can talk to her cats in peace. They often have the most helpful suggestions about difficult cases.
chloestopahunt.net

ERICA WRIGHT is a Tennessee-based PI with a weakness for fried foods. When not chasing a lead, she can be found befriending the local crows and trying not to kill her houseplants.
www.ericawright.org

SIDEKICK BOOKS

is a London-based small press specialising in multi-authored works of amalgamation and defiant experimentation.

10 POETS

is a series of books in which poets are invited to turn their skills to new and surprising ends.

TITLES IN THIS SERIES:

Ten Poets Defend Their Cities from Giant, Strange Beasts
Ten Poets Tell You Their Favourite Ghost Story
Ten Poets Get to the Bottom of Some Grisly Crimes
Ten Poets Charm the Pants off Ten Historical Figures

You might also like to try...

SIDEKICK HEADBOOKS

Headlong expeditions into the half-known, a blend of the factual and fantastical, the lyrical and the visual, left deliberately incomplete – with blank, scrapbook and customisable pages, so that you can make each one your own.

TITLES IN THIS SERIES:

Aquanauts
Bad Kid Catullus
No, Robot, No!
Battalion

You might also like to try...

THE HIPFLASK SERIES

An improvised dance of unusual forms and genres, played out across four collaborative, pocket-sized collections. Each book comprises a selection of works that skirt close to (or cross the border into) poetic composition, revealing the dynamic relationship between poetry and other kinds of writing. The major theme of each is extrapolated from one or other of these key aspects of modern poetry – play, appropriation, subtext *and* conflict *– but the result is a series that occupies its own strange niche: mutant miscellanies, oddball assortments. Good for a nip or a slug or a long, deep swig.*

TITLES IN THIS SERIES:

Roll Again: A Book of Games to Play
You Again: A Book of Love-Hate Stories
Look Again: A Book of Hidden Messages
Say It Again: A Book of Misquotations